Black Creek

+ Bonus flash fiction
ROC-ED

By William Joseph Roberts

Three Ravens Publishing
Chickamauga, GA USA

Ebook ISBN: 978-1-966507-56-7
Trade Paperback ISBN: 978-1-966507-57-4

Black Creek

There are certain things one doesn't tend to forget from their younger years. First kisses, a grandparent's hug, the taste of honey straight from the comb, or the cold chill of death staring back at you from the pitch darkness of an abyss.

I stared at the mine opening. It was cold… Hollow.

The smell of the black damp lingered in the valley, seeping from the maw of the ancient opening.

The weathered keystone still bore the chisel marks of the craftsman who'd carved the numbers "1918" into the stone, the year the mine was opened.

It had been over 30 years since I last saw this place, and it was like time had completely stood still. Other than a little deadfall here and there, it was the same. Spring water trickled from the opening, forming a small, black creek full of coal sediment that ran out of the holler, giving the flowing water its name.

Nothing else had changed, other than I'd grown older.

I whistled that songbird-like tune that had haunted me all of these years.

Phwwwwwhh   weeeet   swwwwwwwwwha Phwwah.

The wind suddenly kicked up, blowing leaves about in a turbulent dust devil of debris. Before the wind died down, I could have sworn I'd heard that tune repeated.

Maybe I wasn't crazy after all.

I whistled again… And there it was like a call and answer tune.

The whistle replied.

It echoed from the dark depths of the mine.

I choked up, fighting to catch my breath.

Chills ran through my body. My stomach heaved, threatening to revolt.

Again, it called; the sound was low and drawn out, pulling at my senses, teasing my fears.

I glanced around. There was no one else there. Nothing, not even squirrels collecting their winter bounty, moved; only a few loose leaves danced about on the wind.

Phwwwwhh   weeeet   swwwwwwwwha Phwwah sounded again. It echoed across the hillsides, but this time, it was followed by low guttural laughter.

Bad Arnold…

This thing had haunted my nightmares for over thirty years. My parents moved us out of state after the courts cleared me of the murder charges. They had to. They were under everyone's watch just as much as I had been.

The therapists over the years repeatedly assured me the memories were nothing more than damp-induced hallucinations; that my friends had fallen victim to the black damp and gotten lost in the abandoned mines.

But I knew better…

I pulled myself together.

I am here for a reason, I reminded myself. I'd never forget their faces. The way that thing had taken my friends one by one that cold October weekend…

The warm orange glow of the oven's element toasted my breakfast and my feet all at the same time. I pulled the blanket tighter around my shoulders and adjusted my feet so the bottoms of my socks didn't burn. It had gotten bad cold, real quick. But that's usually what happened just before Halloween.

That last lingering hint of summer had held on through all of fall to release its stranglehold all of a sudden and let winter take the world in its icy grip.

Mom had the radio playing the WVOW Trading Post. It was a morning ritual followed by most folks that I knew. Especially after Mad Dog Mike Collins had come over from WLOG. As far as I could tell, he had a massive following as a rock jock on the AM station, and that translated into even more listeners on WVOW, the FM station in town, when he started taking on-air calls for the Trading Post.

The latest call in was Hoarse Cat Hatfield. We knew the old timer because he was one of Papaw's drinking buddies from way back when. He lived back in the hills a few hollers over, not too far away from our trailer park. Being a hermit, I was surprised he had access to a phone, but if I had to bet, he was down at Keysers Gas and General Store listening in.

"Well, Hoarse Cat," Mad Dog Mike said, interrupting Hoarse Cat's story of how he'd fell into a yellowjacket nest and needed the cash for medicine. "All of the phone lines are lit up, so you're going to have to get on with it."

"Oh, alright. I've got fifteen pounds of ginseng and three dozen squirrel pelts for sale. Since I need the money quick, I'll take thirty dollars a pound for the seng, and three dollars a pelt. They're all brain-tanned, stretched. and cured right good. Like I said, I could really use the money to get some medicine after falling into that nest."

"Thank you, Hoarse Cat. And how can folks reach you?"

"They can leave a message down here with Mrs. Keyser at Keysers Gas and General Store up near Ethel. She has the goods and knows my prices, so you won't have to wait for me to come back down off the mountain."

"Alright. Thank you, Hoarse Cat. Just to recap, folks. Hoarse Cat has up to fifteen pounds of ginseng at thirty dollars a pound and three dozen squirrel pelts at three dollars a pelt. Just contact Mrs. Keyser at Keysers Gas and General Store up near Ethel. I'm not sure who is game to take up his offer, but that's the first time I've ever heard of someone trading squirrel pelts."

Some of the strangest things came across the Trading Post in the mornings, but pelts were not the strangest thing I'd ever heard by far.

I shivered. A chilly breeze seeped through a hole in the floor by the sink, where the wood had rotted away. I pulled the blanket tighter around myself.

"Mom, why can't we turn on the heat? It's cold."

"Because the oil tank is empty."

"Can't we get more?"

"Yeah, we can. But it won't be till next week after your daddy gets paid."

She grabbed a spatula, plate, and pot holder from the counter. "Move your feet out of the way."

I pulled my feet back from where they were resting on the open oven door, and she pulled the top rack of the oven out to the stops, then scooped my toast and cheese onto the plate and handed it to me.

"Eat your breakfast before it gets cold."

There wasn't anything as great as toast and cheese when we had a block of commodity cheese to use. You know the kind that the government gives out to folks with rice, beans, cornmeal, and such?

I'd gone with Papaw many times to pick up his allotments. Loved a good plate of beans and cornbread too, but there wasn't anything else in this world like a thick slice of that commodity cheese.

Those blocks only lasted so long; not even a full month most times, so I bit into my breakfast and chewed slowly, enjoying the tang of the toasted cheese.

"Don't dawdle," my mom said. "You don't have a lot of time before the bus runs."

She was right. It was already a quarter after six, and I had to be down at the circle—at the mouth of the trailer park before seven. The trailer creaked as she stomped back to the bathroom to get herself ready for work.

I hurried so I wouldn't miss the bus, but not so fast that I couldn't enjoy my breakfast. It was just too good to waste.

The bus pulled up to the stop just as I made it to the circle drive at the end of the trailer park. I ran to make sure I wasn't missed and fell in line with the other kids, bumping into Brian Craddock at the back of the line, who fell forward into James Tabor and Brent Thompson, both of which shoved Craddock back into me. I sidestepped fast enough to miss being stepped on by the mighty mountain giant. Only fourteen years old, Craddock was already six three and two hundred pounds.

There were a large number of kids in the trailer park, but very few were our age. There were a couple of high school seniors and juniors, a handful of younger grade schoolers, then there was our little crew that built dams in the creek, caught crawdads, played kickball, and hung out almost constantly. Besides Craddock, James, and Brent, there was Bubby Shepherd, who lived just across from us. Then there was Danny and Janey Vance, who lived just down the road from the circle along the main road, John Hatfield from a few doors down, and Darlene Browning, who lived directly next door. We were as thick as thieves and as annoying as siblings to each other. But just as soon as anyone messed with any one of us, we were on them like a pack of wild spider monkeys.

That Friday went just like every other Friday for the last several weeks; Dull, boring, and seemed to last forever, especially since the nights were getting darker for longer. But Saturday morning, we were outside playing kickball in the middle of the road before cartoons were even close to being over.

Everyone except Craddock gathered down at the split before the circle, where the road forked. It was nice and wide, with more than enough room for us to play. Someone would grab a piece of gravel or a rock from the creek to mark out the bases on the pavement.

Craddock had went out squirrel hunting before daylight and likely wouldn't be back till later that morning, but that didn't stop the rest of us.

After several games, we grabbed our bikes and rode to Keysers Gas and General Store down by the old Ethel post office for lunch.

Not everyone got an allowance. A few of us did odd jobs and little chores around the trailer park to make a few dollars here and there just to pay for our hot dog habit. I worked for Papaw most of the time till he passed. I still did work around the house for Mamaw, cutting grass, fixing this or that as needed.

Nothing beat one of Mrs. Keyser's church sale hot dogs with a tall bottle of RC cola to wash it down. The best part was we could turn the bottle back in to Mrs. Keyser for a deposit that earned us a nickel each, which was enough for a pack of chewing gum that we shared between us, splitting the sticks as we had to.

"Y'all be good and don't cause no trouble," Mrs. Keyser said as we piled out of the store with our lunches.

"We won't," we replied in unison as we usually did before the door closed on its own behind us.

I plopped myself on the small sidewalk out front of the store and dug in. We'd barely gotten two bites in before Craddock rode up on his bike. He locked the brakes, skidding to a stop on the dusty drive.

"You missed a good game," Brent said. "Danny kicked the ball into the creek again. Almost lost it for good this time."

"Meh." Craddock shrugged, then smiled. "You aren't going to believe the morning I've had." He looked like he was about to burst with excitement.

"Well, did you have any luck this morning?" Danny asked.

"Not really, but you're never going to guess what I found up on the point behind the park."

"A brain cell?" Janey chided.

"What? No." Craddock scowled at her.

"Okay, then what did you find?" I asked.

"An old graveyard."

Brent scoffed. "Okay, so? It's an old graveyard."

"But it's old. Like really, really old."

"Alright, brainiac," Janey continued. "How do you know it's old?"

"Because some of the gravestones is from 1918, and I think some of them have sunk in. I swear I saw a skull looking up at me from one of them. Soon as I found it, I hauled ass back to the house to come find y'all."

"Bullshit." Danny spit on the ground in front of Craddock. "Aint no way. Something that old would have rotted away or been carried off by dogs or something by now."

"Way," Craddock replied.

"What if it's an old Indian burial mound or something?" Bubby asked.

Brent stood and dusted off his rear. "Ooo, what if it is a burial mound and it's full of buried treasure?"

"Like pirate treasure?" Bubby beamed with excitement at the thought.

We all turned to look at Bubby, but Brent was the first to respond. "Does it look like there's an ocean nearby? Why would pirates ever bury their treasure this far up in the mountains? Craddock probably just saw a big round rock or something."

"Come on, y'all." Craddock dropped his bike and shoved Brent. "I know what a skull looks like. It was like Skeletor was staring back at me. And there were stones standing up all around the place.

"Where was that at, Craddock?" Brady Keyser, Mrs. Keyser's son, and the gas pump attendant asked as he hung up the pump nozzle. He pocketed the cash the driver handed him through the passenger window and headed our way.

"What?"

"The graveyard you're talking about. Where was it?"

"Oh, back up on the hill behind the trailer park."

"Wanda or Sunvalley?"

"Sunvalley."

"Was it just up the hill from where Black Creek runs down to meet Dingess Run that flows back along here?" Brady asked, pointing at the creek running behind the store.

"Yeah." Craddock nodded. "That's it."

"Then y'all had best stay away from that graveyard and leave it alone."

"Why's that?"

Brady glanced around at all of us, his eyes wide and wild. "If'n it's the one I think it is, Bad Arnold is buried up there. And that ain't something any of you wanna go messing around with."

"Bad Arnold?"

Brady got anxious all of a sudden, fidgeting and picking at his fingernails while he looked away down the road in thought. I could tell he was fighting with himself over what to say, and turned sheet white before sucking in a shaky breath.

"It ain't a story for me to tell. That's one needs to come from y'all's folks. Just stay away from it. And you'll do it too, if you know what's good for ya." Brady hurried back inside, and I heard the old cash register ding as he opened it to place the money the customer had given him in the till.

Craddock looked over to me. "You ever heard anything about Bad Arnold?"

I shook my head. "Nope. You?"

"Nope," Craddock replied.

"Me neither," Danny added.

"Well, I don't care what he's talking about. I ain't afraid of nothing." Brent puffed out his chest. "I say we go check it out."

"Well, what if it's like Brady said?" Darlene added. "What if it's something we don't want nothing to do with?"

"I'd ask Papaw about it if he were still around," I said. "He seemed to know everything there was to know about…well, everything."

"Then who do we ask? My daddy won't be home from work till late tonight," Craddock said.

I snapped my fingers at a thought. "I bet I know who'd know something about Bad Arnold and that graveyard."

Janey stood, dusting herself off. "Who?"

"Hoarse Cat."

"Who?" Several of the group asked.

"Hoarse Cat. The old timer that lives up there on the mountain," I said, pointing toward the mouth of Bearwallow Holler. He comes down here to the bottom and does his trading with Mrs. Keyser. Me and Papaw used to take him things every now and then, back before he passed away.

"Why do they call him Hoarse Cat?"

"Because he sounds like a Hoarse Cat when he talks, all raspy and growly."

"Wait," Craddock interrupted. "Are you talking about the old hermit that lives up at the head of Bearwallow, back behind the slate dump?"

"Him?" Brent scowled at the thought. "He ain't nothing but a crazy old man. My mom said he lost his marbles years ago."

I laughed. "Hoarse Cat may seem crazy, but he's been around these parts longer than my Mamaw and Papaw, or anyone else I know of, for that matter, except for maybe Mrs. Keyser. I'd be willing to bet he's been around longer than anyone else in the trailer park. He might know a thing or two. I've gone up there to his cabin a few times with Papaw to carry vegetables from the garden to him. They'd sit and talk for hours, telling stories and sipping on whatever Papaw brought along with him. And let me tell you, some of the stories he told were almost unbelievable."

Danny stood and shrugged. "I ain't got anything else better to do."

"Then let's go." I stood, quickly finishing my dog before I drained my bottle of RC.

We hurried to return our deposits in trade for gum, then jumped on our bikes and headed up the rough dirt road that led into Bearwallow Holler and the old slate dump. How Hoarse Cat could stand to be around this place most days, I didn't understand.

Papaw told me that the slate dump was where the local mines dumped all the slag, slate, and unwanted coal to get it out of the way after they'd sorted it from the good stuff.

At some point, the dump had caught fire and has been burning to some degree since. Most days it wasn't bad, but there were days when the air got so thick with the stink of sulfur it hung heavy in the air and got into everything. On the really bad days, a cloud of low-hanging smoke rolled down from Bearwallow and hovered over the bottom, giving the whole area an eerie feel like out of some B-rate horror flick. Luckily, today it wasn't bad at all, and a decent breeze blew down off the mountain.

It took us almost an hour to get to the head of Bearwallow Holler before we hiked up the hillside to where Hoarse Cat had his *cabin*, which was more or less just a rough-built shed made from scraps of this, that, or whatever he could get a hold of.

Hoarse Cat was nothing if not resourceful. He'd built a small fireplace and chimney out of mountain stone and clay he'd dug out of the hillside and survived mostly off the land by trapping and foraging. I did not doubt that if anyone knew anything about things in these hills, it would be the old hermit, especially Bad Arnold.

The abandoned mine road we'd been walking on continued along the hillside and crossed over the ridgeline another three hundred yards ahead. Hoarse Cat's cabin sat almost directly uphill from where we stood on the overgrown road. He'd built it into a rock outcropping close to the ridgeline, maybe another hundred yards or so uphill from where we stood.

It was off the beaten path to say the least.

I spotted several deer paths crisscrossing the hillside, but nothing that looked like it had been worn down by major foot traffic.

Craddock huffed. "Why the hell does he live so far back here?"

"He doesn't exactly like people. I know that much," I answered.

"I don't like people either," Brent said, "but you don't see me hiding back in the hills like some kinda caveman."

John stopped, resting with his hands on his knees. "He could have at least built it closer toward the bottom of the hill."

I laughed. "I think that's the whole point of being this far back on the mountain. Come on. We don't have much further to go."

John nodded, then turned, falling back in line with the rest of us as he continued uphill. We'd continued maybe another fifty yards when Craddock tripped, setting off a clattering racket that exploded all around us.

Craddock let out a panicked scream. "Get it off, get it off, get it off!" He kicked at something wrapped around his foot, and the cacophony of noise grew with each flailing kick.

Every one of us froze, blood chilled at the sound of a gunshot that rang out from uphill. James let out a high-pitched cry.

"Y'all are trespassing!" a voice shouted from uphill. "Get off my mountain!"

I stood and cupped my hands around my mouth. "Hoarse Cat! It's me! Wayne! Hassle's grandson."

"Who?" I could see him now, standing in the doorway of his cabin, cupping a hand around his left ear.

"It's me! Wayne!"

He stepped fully out of the cabin and stood on the stoop of the entrance. He shaded his eyes, trying to get a better look at us. "What in the world are you bunch doing, traipsing up this way? Don't you know there's things out in these hills that will eat a bunch of youngins like you?"

Darlene cried. Janey pulled her close, holding her in a hug to comfort her.

James turned to me. "What does he mean something out here will eat us?"

I shrugged. "Like you didn't know there were bears and bobcats in these hills."

"That old man is crazy. You sure he isn't going to eat us? Maybe he was actually threatening us?"

I shushed them. "He's no crazier than any of us. He just prefers to live a little differently. Don't go and get him riled up, or he'll never answer anything for us. He's…" I started and stopped, thinking of the right word. "Hoarse Cat is fickle, and will swing with whatever way the mood takes him. Now hush before you ruin our chances."

Cupping my hands, I shouted uphill once more. "We wanted to ask you some questions. Figured you knew a thing or two, and you'd be the best person to ask."

He shifted uncomfortably, like he wasn't sure what to make of what I'd said. Then it almost looked like he was arguing with himself.

Hoarse Cat cupped his hands around his mouth and shouted back. "What'd you bring me in trade?"

"Trade?" Someone said. We all looked back and forth to each other, hoping for an answer. I shrugged.

"What do you mean trade?"

Hoarse Cat chuckled. "You come up here wanting something, you gotta bring something in trade. One thing for another, you know? That's just how it is. Didn't your papaw teach you anything, boy?"

"Shit," I said, forgetting one of the most important parts of our visits with Hoarse Cat. Papaw would bring him supplies or other odds and ends in trade for things like ginseng, sassafras, yellow root, and other things he'd forage from the woods.

"What are we going to do?" Brent asked.

"Well," I said, thinking. I looked around at our little group. "What does everyone have?"

Danny looked taken aback. "What? I'm not giving up anything."

"You gotta, or we came all this way for nothing." I removed my ball cap and held it out like a beggar's cup.

"Everyone, empty your pockets," Janey ordered.

"Screw you. Ain't no way," Craddock replied.

Janey let out a frustrated growl. "Do it, Craddock, or so help me–I'll tell your daddy what I caught you doing behind the shed this past summer."

"What? Wait? You wouldn't…"

She crossed her arms and glared up at him, impatiently tapping her fingers. "Okay, okay." Craddock reached into his pockets, dropping the contents into my cap.

"The same goes for the rest of you," she continued. "I'm cold, tired, and just want to go home." She poked her walking stick into Danny's chest. "Come on."

He swatted at her stick and dug into his pockets. "Alright, alright. Geez."

"Well, I'm waiting," Hoarse Cat shouted. The rest joined in and started to empty what they had into my cap.

"Alright, hang on. We're working on it!"

I sorted through the pile dropped into the cap: Acorns, paperclips, ball bearings, and a mix of other odds and ends. I pulled together three dollars in change, a half-empty package of chewing gum, and the old timer pocket knife my papaw had given me. It wasn't much for size, but it made up for that by being useful more times than I could count.

Hoarse Cat stood, tiptoing and craning his neck to see what he could. "An old man ain't got all day. Death is just around the corner, and I ain't got no time to waste on y'all."

"Wait, I think I got it," I shouted. "Three and a half dollars, two sticks of chewing gum, and my Old Timer pocket knife, Papaw gave me. It's all we've got with us of value."

"Oh," Hoarse Cat piped up, and let out a long, thoughtful laugh. "That might just do it. Y'all come on up here and let me take a look."

"Come on," I said, hurrying up the hillside. "Let's go before he changes his mind."

"But," Bubby started, "what if he wants to eat us?"

Brent laughed. "Come on, you big baby." Craddock bumped him as they walked by.

"You can always walk back on your own," Danny said, shrugged, and continued up the hill.

Visiting the small cabin was always a treat. It never failed that I'd spot something new and different I hadn't seen before. Hoarse Cat had a bad habit of *collecting* what other people considered to be trash when he thought it had some value or use. Most of it was broken trash and littered the area around the cabin. But there were those few select treasures that he kept inside among the animal pelts, drying ginseng, and wild onions.

Hoarse Cat stoked his fire as we piled into the cabin. He dropped in a large chunk of coal that quickly ignited, then pulled a small pot away from the hot coals and poured it into half of an old beer can that had been cut in two and the ragged edge folded over, making a smooth lip.

"Any of you want a little birch bark tea?" Everyone silently shook their heads. "Hrumf. Suit yourselves. Just more for me." He shrugged, took a drink, and held out his hand toward me.

"Well?"

"Oh, the trade. Yeah," I said, and handed him the gathered payment.

He set down his tea and chuckled, sorting through the coins with a dirty finger, then pocketed the lot. He oddly stared at the pocket knife. "You said your papaw gave this to you?"

"Yes, sir. For my tenth birthday."

Hoarse Cat passed the knife back to me. "Wouldn't want to get your papaw upset at you then." He flashed a crooked-tooth smile then leaned back in his seat. "So, how come y'all come all the way up here?"

We all looked at each other, waiting for someone else to say the first word.

Hoarse Cat looked from one person to the next. "Don't you know, I don't have time to waste on nonsense. I've got things to get done. The cold months are on top of us, and I've already got too much to get done before the snow comes. Or did you just come up here, funning me? Trying to get me to waste my time?"

He gasped. A look of paranoid confusion danced across his face.

"Or are you bunch trying to distract me?" He grabbed up an old, worn double-barreled shotgun. "Ain't no one gonna find my honey holes without a fight. That's my ginseng, you hear?"

"Hoarse Cat," I called, pulling his attention. He turned back to me, and a low rumbly growl escaped his throat.

"No one is here to take your ginseng," I said. "We're here to find out about Bad Arnold."

The old Hermit froze at the mention of the name. He'd suddenly gone sheet white, and his eyes glistened in the dim firelight.

"What's wrong, Hoarse Cat? Are you okay? Did I say something wrong?"

"Bad Arnold," he hoarsely whispered. He sucked in a ragged breath and licked his lips, pulling himself together.

"Bad Arnold is something you kids want to stay as far away from as possible. It ain't nothing but bad juju. Always has been, always will be. Y'all stay the hell away from it and never mention that name again if you know what's good for you."

Every one of us exchanged confused glances. No one else seemed ready to step up to the plate, so I pressed on.

"But why?" I asked him. "Brady down at the gas station said something similar when Craddock mentioned finding a graveyard up on the hillside."

Hoarse Cat became visibly agitated at the mention of the graveyard. He scratched long grooves in the grime covering his forearms and quietly thought for another moment before he spoke again.

"You boys ain't been up there, have you?" Tears started to well up in his eyes, and his face twisted. He became visibly distressed, a whimper escaping as he fought to keep it together. "Please tell me you haven't been up to the graveyard."

"I was up there squirrel hunting this morning," Craddock admitted.

Hoarse Cat let out a high-pitched wail. "Are you boys trying to bring the Pale

Horseman himself down on us? You don't go messing around with that graveyard, that mine, or so help me you'll unleash Bad Arnold on us again."

"Mine?" Someone asked

We couldn't make it any worse than it was, so I poked him a little more. "What do you mean, *again*, Hoarse Cat?"

Hoarse Cat froze. If his sharp glare were a blade, it would have carved its way right through me.

"Yes," he growled matter-of-factly. "Again." He suddenly fought for breath, each one coming in panicked gasps that he slowly forced under control by nothing more than a pure force of will.

"But *what* happened, Hoarse Cat?"

"You'd think other folks would remember and tell their youngins and grandyoungins about what happened to us back in '56. No one remembers, or maybe they just don't want to remember."

"1956?" Bubby asked with a gasp. "That's forever ago."

Hoarse Cat continued. "No one ever believed me. Anytime it did get brought up, they just called me crazy."

"So, you know who Bad Arnold is?"

Hoarse Cat whimpered, breathing forcefully through his nose, snot shot out of his left nostril, and clung to his scruffy mustache. He fought back against what I expected to be a full-blown crying fit at this point. Pulling himself together, he nodded and let out a reluctant, "Yes."

Setting back in his seat, he clutched the shotgun to his chest, hugging it like it was his favorite teddy bear. Most of our group shifted uncomfortably. Craddock and John inched closer to the door.

"Who was he?" Janey asked in a sweet, caring tone. Hoarse Cat whimpered. His eyes watered, a single tear escaped, leaving a clean line down his grubby cheek. He took in a shuddering breath and slowly shook his head side to side

"Please, no…"

"But we came all this way." Bubby, the smallest of the group, said.

"Yeah, we'd really like to know why we shouldn't go near there," Darlene added.

"Please, Horse Cat. You know Papaw would have told me if he were still alive."

The old mountain man's lower lip quivered. The pain of memories flooding back twisted his face. Tears freely flowed, washing away what looked like ages of dirt and grime.

"He might have…" Hoarse Cat gasped for breath, nodding slowly to himself. "He might have told you if you'd asked him. He was there with me. But he wouldn't ever talk about it. It was just too hard for him." He looked up at us with pleading eyes. "It was our fault Sadie and the others died. I know it was."

"Why?" Danny asked. "What makes you think that?"

Hoarse Cat drifted off in thought once again, then mumbled something so low it was probably meant more to himself than any of us. "I can still hear his voice…" He parted his lips and tried to whistle, then swallowed hard. "Dig… I can still hear his voice saying that word over and over, like he's standing right there next to you." He sucked in a breath. "And the sound of that incessant tune he whistled…"

The old timer shook his head and whinced.

"It's okay, Hoarse Cat," I said. "We're here with you."

He fought back another sobbing fit and composed himself.

"Cecile and Dewy messed with some of the gravestones up on that hill," he continued. They kicked over a few, broke a few." He shrugged. "They weren't much, really. There were a few fancy ones someone had bought in town, but most were either chunks of mountain stone or hunks of slate from the mine, carved with a name and date.

We even found a skull half-buried in the dirt in one of the sunken graves."

"But what does that have to do with Sadie and the others?" I asked.

Anger contorted his face, scowling up at me. "Ain't you been listening, boy? Cause Bad Arnold took them."

His whole body shook, sobbing harder than I'd ever seen anyone sob before. Reaching over with a shaky hand, he drank down the rest of his tea and began again.

"Sadie screamed for so long. We couldn't find her. No idea where Bad Arnold had taken her. We'd heard a scuffle behind us, and by the time we could turn, we barely caught sight of an old, ragged miner dragging Cecil and Dewy away into the dark of that damned mine. Just like that," he said with a snap, "they were gone." He took another deep breath and stared off into nothing like the devil himself was standing there in front of us.

"Bad Arnold strangled Shawn right there in front of us. Forced him to his knees, demanding we get back to work... The carts won't fill themselves... The company has a quota to keep…"

"But her screams…"

"Her screams echoed in that labyrinth. They seemed to come from everywhere at the same time."

"We looked… We looked for so long… We tried to find her…" He quietly sobbed for another moment. "I swear we tried to find her. We were down there for days before we found our way out—feeling along cold, damp walls that all felt exactly the same as the rest. Our flashlights had given out by the end of the first day, and it didn't take long before we were turned around.

"Hassel's mamma was beside herself with grief so bad she just gave up. She stopped eating… stopped caring. It wasn't no time before she got sick and just died."

Hoarse Cat anxiously twisted the barrel of the gun in his hands so hard I could hear his skin pulling on the cold steel.

"His daddy never did forgive him. Everyone blamed us for letting Sadie and the others get lost in that mine. There were dozens of miners got together and went down there to search, but no one found anything. Just rusted equipment, and a few piles of deer bones they'd figured were from a bear or mountain lion that had used the mine as a den. They said a lot of the tunnels had collapsed and flooded. Which made a lot of sense." He shrugged again, nodding to himself before he continued.

"My Paw told me it was a really old mine. Opened by the Aracoma Mining company back in the early 19 aughts or so. They figured the damp had probably gotten to Sadie and our friends, and they'd most likely fallen down a flooded shaft. That's why they said no one could find their bodies."

"So, who was Bad Arnold?" Janey asked in probably the softest, most caring tone I'd ever heard her use.

Hoarse Cat took another deep breath, then forcefully huffed like a weightlifter. "My Paw'd told me Bad Arnold was a miner, back when the mine first opened. He'd worked for years, digging that dark black coal by hand and loading it into the mule-drawn push carts. That's where the creek got its name, because of all the coal dust that washed down the holler from the mine. Then, after the previous mine super died, the company made Bad Arnold the new mine supervisor.

He was cruel to the other miners, running them like a slave crew. He'd beat them if they got behind schedule. Paw said Bad Arnold worked those miners to death because the Aracoma Coal Company had quotas. And by the power of the company, Bad Arnold ruled with an iron fist."

Hoarse Cat visibly relaxed the more he talked. Loosening his grip on the shotgun, he leaned back in his chair.

"Well," I said, now curious about where he was going with his story. "What happened?"

"The miners went on strike. They refused to mine another pound of coal until the Company replaced Bad Arnold. When they walked out and stated their demands, Bad Arnold shot the ring leader, Tennis Vance, if I remember Paw correctly. Little man, but meaner than a pissed-off copperhead when you got him riled up. He'd gotten fed up with the way they were being treated and rallied the men for the strike."

Hoarse Cat picked up his makeshift cup and shook a few droplets into his mouth, huffed, then held the cup out and waggled it at me. I stepped over to the fire and poured him another cup before he continued.

"Bad Arnold expected them to turn tail and go back to work when he stepped out with his shotgun and the company's hired Pinkerton's backing him, but they did just the opposite.

I shifted, looking back at the others, then turned back to Hoarse Cat. "What do you mean?"

Hoarse Cat took another drink, sat back, and relaxed a bit more. "Those men had been pushed to their limits. They tore Bad Arnold apart; took their time, too. Each of them taking their turn at him before they hooked him up to the mules and ripped him apart.

"Is that why he's up there in that graveyard?" Craddock asked, chiming in.

Hoarse Cat nodded. "Most of the miners in those days weren't from around here. They'd come because of promises of work and taken whatever they could find when they got here, for better or worse. Most made the trip with nothing to start with, so they had no choice but to take the work. They didn't have anything when they got here either, and became beholden to the company store. They'd send whatever cash or goods they could back to their families, but that was after the company took their cut of the pay."

"The Company had graveyards all over these hills, full of miners, usually just up the hill from the mine entrance. They'd put the man in a pine box if he were lucky, carry them up the hill, and say a few words before returning them to the earth. My Paw said that particular graveyard, where Bad Arnold was buried, was full of blacks. Bunch of them come north to get away from the fields down south and died in a roof fall just after the mine opened. Those men probably had it better than the ones that worked under Bad Arnold," he said, then drifted off into thought once again.

He tried to whistle again, then licked his lips and let out a low, birdlike call. He sobbed, clutching his arms around himself.

"We should probably get going," Craddock nervously said and headed out the door.

I didn't think Craddock was wrong. Hoarse Cat curled up in his chair and buried his face into a threadbare cushion before he broke down and began bawling.

"Yeah," I added. "I think Craddock is right. We should probably get going. Thank you, Hoarse Cat. You take care of yourself." I hurried through the cobbled-together door with the others and caught up to Craddock.

Craddock looked shaken.

"What's wrong?" I asked.

Craddock chin-nodded back toward the shack. "What Hoarse Cat whistled."

"Yeah, what about it?"

"Sounded like a bird call to me," someone else added.

"I swear I heard that exact tune this morning when I was up at the graveyard."

"Aw, you're full of it," Danny said.

"Yeah," James added.

"No, I'm not. It's the truth," Craddock insisted.

"Then let's go back up there," Brent urged.

"I dunno," Craddock said, taking a step back. "Didn't you hear what he said?"

"He's just a crazy old man," Brent said, waving off the thought.

Craddock turned to me. "What do you think, Wayne?"

"Dunno." I shrugged. I looked up to see the sun still fairly high in the sky. "Still plenty of daylight left. We could make it up there and back before dark."

"Sounds good to me," Danny added.

"Y'all are on your own," Janey said. "I have a book and a warm blanket calling my name. I'm going home." She started her way down the hill.

"Hang on, I'll go with you," Bubby shouted, following close on her heels.

"Bubby, where you going?"

"Home…" was the only thing we could hear him say as he ran down the hillside ahead of Janey.

"Well," Brent nervously laughed. "Who's up for a hike?"

"I really don't know, guys," Craddock replied, backing away. He held up his hands defensively. "What if it gets dark before we can get off the hill?"

I looked up again. "We've got a few hours at least."

"But what if?"

"Alright," Danny began. "So we all run home, grab flashlights and whatever else we need, and meet back at Craddocks."

"What?" Craddock squeaked.

We ran most of the way to the bottom of the mountain before getting back to where we'd left our bikes. Luckily, it was mostly downhill the whole way, making the trek out that much easier. I ran home, grabbed my backpack, some snacks, a flashlight, and filled my canteen. It couldn't have been more than an hour from when we'd left Hoarse Cat's before I was walking up to Craddock's trailer. Brent, Danny, Darlene, James, and John milled about in the yard by the front door.

"We ready?" I asked.

"It took you long enough," Danny said, turning to me. "See if you can talk some sense into Craddock."

"What's wrong?"

"He's a big chicken," Brent added. Darlene started clucking like a chicken on cue.

"Yeah," John shouted, clucking along with Darlene. "Come on out, you yellow-bellied sissy."

"Chicken shit. Chicken shit." James and Brent chanted in unison, and a few of the others joined in.

"Come on, Craddock," I shouted. "You gotta go and show us. You're the one that's been up to the graveyard."

A muffled, "But what about Bad Arnold?" Came from inside the trailer.

"It's just a story," Brent shouted. "The old man is crazy."

"But I kicked one of the headstones."

"So," James shouted back. "It's a dirty old headstone. I want to see that skull."

"I do too," John added. "Come on, already. Let's go."

"Come on, Craddock," I shouted. "The first sign of trouble and we haul ass down the hill."

"What makes you think we can outrun Bad Arnold?"

"If we can outrun a black bear, we can outrun a ghost," Brent replied.

The door cracked open, slowly. "You think so?"

"Makes sense to me," Danny said.

"You promise?"

"Yup," I said. "Now let's go before we waste any more time hem hawing around."

It easily took us over an hour to hike the ridgeline, crossing over boulders and fighting our way through bramble thorns before we reached the graveyard. The area was more or less flat and level, with stones scattered haphazardly about near several depressions in the ground. Nature had reclaimed most of the graveyard. Trees and bramble vines had overgrown most of the area.

One of the times I'd gone with Papaw to clean off the family graveyard, he'd pointed out several spots to me where the ground had sunken in. He told me how older graves would do that because the pine boxes had rotted and collapsed, causing the dirt above to sink and fill in the void over time.

"Well," I said, turning to Craddock. "It looks just like you said."

Brent, Danny, and John were already wandering about, reading off the names and dates that were still legible.

"Where was the skull?" James asked.

"Just over there," Craddock answered. Reluctantly pointing down the side of the ridgeline.

Brent nudged Craddock as he walked past. "Come on, chicken. What are you scared of?"

"Yeah, chicken. It's just a skull," James added.

I stood next to Craddock, and we slowly followed the others. "Why aren't you up there with them? Don't you want to see a skull up close?" he asked.

"Yeah, seen them plenty of times," I absentmindedly answered.

"Oh, yeah?" Brent asked, turning on me. "When was this?"

"Whenever Big Dan dug up the hole where he normally buries the leftover bits when they're slaughtering hogs.

They dump the guts, skin, and head in there. Papaw would keep the head for the jowl meat and to make head cheese sometimes, but no one else wanted it after he passed away, so they'd just toss it in the hole with the rest."

"Holy, shit," John shouted. "Hey guys, you gotta come see this." He excitedly waved us over.

We hurried over the hillside and found John squatting at the edge of a sunken grave. Sure enough, at the far end of the depression was a sun-bleached skull like you'd see in the movies that stared up into the sky, but it was still partially buried in the dirt.

Brent pushed his way past John and dropped down into the depression. "So, Mister Skully, who exactly might you be?"

"Hey, now," I shouted. "Don't you know you ain't supposed to step on graves? It's disrespectful and bad luck."

"Mind your own business." Brent waved off the thought and turned back to the skull.

"I bet it's plastic and someone just put it there," Danny said, then dropped down beside Brent and pried the skull from the dirt with a stick. He turned it over so the two of them could examine it.

"Dunno," Brent said. "It doesn't look like plastic."

"Maybe it is real."

Brent started to dig with the stick Danny had used. "I wonder if there's any treasure in here with him? You know, like a tomb."

"That makes you a grave robber, dumbass," I said.

Brent shrugged. "So? It ain't like he needs it anymore," he said, nodding toward the skull.

Darlene flipped over a broken piece of slate from the head of the depression. "Hey, this has something carved into it."

"That's the one I kicked when I was out here hunting," Craddock said. "It was already partially broken. I didn't see the skull till after I kicked it. Thought it was kinda odd sitting there sticking out of the ground like it was."

"Did you read it before you kicked it?" I shoved Craddock.

"I didn't see any writing on it. I just saw a rock."

"Flip over the rest of it and see what it says," James suggested, and hurried around the hole toward Darlene.

They flipped over the pieces and placed them back together on the ground like a large puzzle, then Darlene let out a sudden gasp.

James backpeddled, falling backward onto Danny and Brent.

"What is it?" I asked.

Darlene stared back at us, wide-eyed and pale. She swallowed hard. "Arnold Meadows, 1922."

Craddock whispered, "Bad Arnold," almost too quiet to be heard.

Crows cawed from somewhere down the slope, then the wind suddenly gusted without warning. Dust and leaves swirled around in a flurry that died down almost as fast as it had appeared.

"Get off me," Danny shouted, shoving James away. Brent, Danny, and James scrambled out of the depression. The skull lay there, discarded where it had been dropped. It stared back at us with its empty, hollow eyes.

Phwwwwwhh weeeet swwwwwwwwwha Phwwah whistled among the trees, but it wasn't like any bird song I'd ever heard.

The high-pitched shrill repeated again, reverberating on the wind as if the sound floated through the forest on aethereal wings.

"What was that?" Darlene asked.

Panic quickly set in. Leaves erupted again in a whirlwind all around us. That's when I noticed the skull. Those two empty black sockets glowed a deep crimson, darker than the color of fresh blood that swirled like two whirlpools to hell. The wind gusted stronger than I'd ever felt before.

"Dig," a voice commanded, surrounding us. The wind gusted harder, nearly knocking me to the ground.

"Bad Arnold," Craddock screamed. He turned to run and stumbled, rolling down the hillside.

"Run," I shouted, then sprinted down the slope right behind Craddock. I slid downhill on the sides of my feet through the damp leaf litter covering the hillside. Grabbing saplings as I went, I controlled my descent, shifting from one side to the other like a downhill skier.

I glanced back to see the others following, each of them working their way down the slope as fast as they could.

"Dig…" the ghostly voice commanded, followed by that incessant whistling.

Wind rushed downhill, gusting, bending, doubling over saplings. It forced us along faster. I tumbled forward, sliding face down in the dirt for several feet.

Others tumbled past me to the bottom of the holler. What had taken us over an hour to hike up to the ridgeline, we'd descended in minutes down the steep slopes of the hillside.

"Dig…" the voice raged.

Dark clouds covered the sky. Smokey mist roiled up the holler toward us that pulsed the same dark crimson swirling in the skull's eye sockets..

"Dig…"

"What do we do?" Brent shouted. Panic-stricken, he grabbed me by the shoulders and shook me. "We have to get out of here."

"Come on, this way!" I turned to see Danny, James, and John already running up the holler, away from the smoke.

"The trailer park is the other way," I shouted after them.

Danny turned back to me and pointed uphill. "We can cross the next ridgeline and come out near Bearwallow again," he called back.

Darlene shrugged. "It's as good a plan as any," she said and sprinted away following the two of them.

"Dig…" the voice roared. Screams of agonizing pain erupted from behind me. I spun to look, but ready to run. Craddock knelt in the cloud of approaching smoke, his arms spread like they were being pulled upward and outward.

I'd never heard anyone scream like that before. Part pain, part panicked fear. His clothes, hair, and skin all began to smolder as the smoke enveloped him. It flickered and flashed with the same crimson hue.

Above and behind Craddock amid the conflagration, I saw what looked like two dark swirling eyes emerge. They hung ten feet or more in the air and gazed down at Craddock like a dragon examining a sacrificial offering. Craddock's screaming stopped, and his head fell limp against his chest. I could hear the crackling pop of flesh and tendons being torn apart just before Craddock's arms were wrenched from their sockets.

"RUN!"

James tripped, entangled in a bramble vine bush that began to snake around his limbs, wrapping them tight. Blood soaked into his clothes, seeping from the hundreds of thorns piercing through his clothing.

"Help me!"

Fumbling for my pocket knife I stopped to cut him loose, then watched in horror as ground opened up and the bramble vines pulled James down into the dark opening in the earth, engulfing him in seconds.

I set off at a full sprint, following the others upstream along the banks of a small dark creek. The walls of an abandoned stone building came into sight. Danny and Brent ran around to the front and skidded to a sudden stop.

Danny kicked at something that flopped and fell to the ground. "The doors are rotted off."

We all rushed into the skeletal remains of the building and hunkered down behind the stone wall. Large portions of the roof had collapsed into the large room, rotten from decades of neglect and decay.

The smoke enveloped the area, blocking off our escape on either hillside. The leaves and trees all around smoldered, giving off an acrid, sulfurous stench.

"Where's James?" someone asked.

Bracing myself against my knees, I fought to catch my breath, slowing each panted breath before I spoke up.

"The ground just opened up and swallowed him whole."

"Shit," Danny cursed.

"We gotta hide or run."

"Run where?" Darlene slapped me across the back of the head. "The only place to run is the mine."

"No way I'm going into that mine," Brent said, then peeked around the corner of the stone wall.

"Then what?" Danny shouted. "Where else can we go? It ain't like we can sprout wings and fly away."

"Why is everything smoking? Is it burning?" Darlene shuddered and wrapped her arms around herself tightly.

"I don't know, but I sure as hell don't want to find out," Danny said, and turned Darlene to face him. "Have you ever been in a mine before?"

Her tight brunette curls shook furiously. Her voice cracked as she began to answer him.

"N...n...no. Never."

Danny held her shoulders firm so she couldn't sprint away like a frightened deer.

I grabbed his arm and spun him around. "Are you crazy? You can't go in there. It'll be like shooting fish in a barrel for Bad Arnold if you step into that mine. Didn't you hear what Hoarse Cat said? Bad Arnold ran that mine."

His jaw muscles clenched as he chewed on the thought for a second, letting out a low growl between clenched teeth before he spoke again. "We don't have a choice," he said matter-of-factly, then turned back to Darlene.

"We get in there, you have to hold on to my belt, don't let go. You don't want to get separated." Darlene nodded as furiously as she had shaken her head moments before.

"If you do, just call out, I'll stop and backtrack to you. My older cousin told me that these old mines are all connected. If we're lucky, we can cross over through one of the older connections and make it out through the Ethel Holler entrance on the other side. We're only a few miles from there, and that's nothing compared to the ground we cover on a normal day."

"You're crazy," I muttered, taking a step back from Danny.

He turned, "Not as crazy as you if you think you can outrun it. Look around. It's surrounding us. Do you really want to try to sprint uphill through that?"

"What if we can kill it?" Brent asked.

Danny turned on Brent, glaring at him, nose to nose. "How? Cause I'm all ears."

"A cross, or we cast it out with the power of Jesus," Darlene added.

Brent laughed. "You really think Jesus is going to do anything here?"

"There has to be something," I pleaded.

"If you fall in the smoke, you'll burn. Look at what happened to Cradock. The safest thing is to run through the mine, and that's exactly what I plan to do. Anyone who wants to survive, come with me."

The world around us erupted in a cacophony of debris and wind.

"We gotta go," Danny shouted and grabbed Darlene by the wrist.

I shoved him, breaking his grip on her wrist. "What if it'll pass over us?"

"After what it already did, do you really think it'll pass over us?"

"*Dig…*" reverberated through the holler, the words echoing in my skull.

He was right. We were all standing around the grave when they picked up the skull. It wanted all of us. More bodies for the mine. More workers for the company. Bad Arnold wouldn't stop till he had all of us.

"Fine," I shouted over the roar of the wind. "But we stick together. Just like the Musketeers, all for one, and one for all!"

"Deal!" Danny grabbed my hand and shook, then did the same with Brent and John before he turned and took Darlene's hand into his, getting ready to sprint for the mine entrance.

Danny glanced back at us, then took a deep breath.

"Go!" He sprinted ahead, Darlene in tow, stumbling behind him.

Shadowy hands reached out from the smoke, poking and prodding at them as they raced for the entrance. Darlene slipped, falling face-first to the ground.

"Don't leave me," she screamed, her voice shrill and panicked. Danny turned and grabbed her arm, fighting against the grasp of the dark hands as they began dragging her away by her ankles.

I froze, gooseflesh rippling across my skin, the hairs on the back of my neck rose like a dog's hackles. My limbs refused to respond as I watched the thing attacking Darlene.

John and Brent rushed ahead, grabbing hold of her arms, and the three of them fought with all their strength against the shadowy grip.

A deep and guttural, "*Dig…*" echoed through the holler, shaking the stone floor beneath my feet when another spectral hand appeared in the doorway of the ruined building. It floated there just inside the opening, swaying to the left of the entrance like campfire smoke drifting on the wind.

It must have heard my short panting breaths over the gusting wind. The smoking hand suddenly turned, lunging for me.

Ducking under a rotten roof beam, partially leaning against the wall, I scrambled back to my feet and rushed to the rear of the building. Fallen debris and overgrown vegetation blocked the rear exit.

The shadowy hand pressed forward, coming for me. Evil laughter clung to the air. I kicked at the leaves covering the floor, looking for anything I could use as a weapon, when my foot struck something hard that tinked like metal on stone.

Frantic, I ducked as it grasped at me, quickly digging a large metal pry bar from the debris. It was heavy, but not so heavy that I couldn't lift it. I stabbed upward with it in a desperate strike.

A bestial rumble emanated from the shadow. It flailed and yanked its smoky form from the rust-covered point of the bar. As it retreated, a man-like form began to form

I advanced, stabbing the bar at the shadowman like a caveman with a spear. Again, it stepped back in retreat.

Something in me said I could kill it. I could save us all. Charging forward, I plunged the bar into the center of the creature's body. It howled in pain and dispersed in a literal puff of smoke. Had I just killed it? Had I killed Bad Arnold or some other demon?

"Don't let it take me!"

Darlene…

Rushing through the doorway, I sprinted toward the others, bar in hand and ready to strike.

"Hold it! I know how to kill it!" The others looked at me like I was some sort of madman.

Swinging with all my might, the bar cut through the ghostly appendage and poofed from existence, its mass dragging me along with it to the ground.

"Run," I shouted, scrambling to my feet as I pushed past the others.

"Get back to work!" The beast roared, and the entire holler shook with rage. I glanced back in time to see something large and dark forming deep in the smoke.

Those eyes swayed back and forth, closing the distance between us from the darkness. The ragged figure of a man emerged.

"Dig…" it rasped. Smoke belched forth from his mouth with the word.

Bad Arnold… I hadn't killed him.

The figure reared its hand back with a bullwhip and cracked it in our direction, striking John across the back of his left arm. Blood pooled on the ground at his feet, flowing freely from the wound.

We scattered. Racing through the thick undergrowth that had reclaimed the area.

John let out a gurgled scream. I turned in time to see Bad Arnold yank John from his feet, the end of the whip wrapped around his neck.

He kicked and flailed like a pissed off two year old, fighting to free himself. His grunted gasps reminded me of a bulldog with allergies chowing down on Gravy Train kibble. Tendrils of smoke snaked out from his clothes and flesh as they smoldered, adding to the roiling smoke surrounding us.

The whip shot out again, knocking the bar free from my hand.

I turned and sprinted, following Brent into another small stone structure to the left of the mine entrance. The roof of the building had partially collapsed, covering the top of a massive fan that took up the other half of the building.

"Come on, we can hide in here." Brent hurried, climbing through an open access hatch on the side of the fan.

Tendrils of mist seeped into the building, creeping across the stone floor like a slithering serpent.

I followed quickly behind Brent, sliding beneath the massive scroll fan wheel inside the housing as he climbed upward through a rusted-out gap between the blades of the old mine fan. Cracked stone and soil littered the bottom of the fan housing. I could make out a cubby through the rusted hole in the back of the housing. I squirmed under the wheel and found the space was where the shaft bearing was mounted, cradled in a cutout within the stone. A thin sliver of light leaking through a crack in the cubby disrupted the darkness.

I army crawled through the dirt and grime into the cubby and sat up, my back against the stone wall. The top looked to be a heavy metal grate covered in debris.

Peeking out of the crack, I watched Danny and Darlene run into the opening of the mine.

"No," I whispered to myself. "Stupid, stupid, stupid, stupid."

"Dig…"

I clasped a hand over my mouth and froze. The sound of my heartbeat pounded in my ears.

Rusty gears squeaked and rattled as the fan wheel started to shift, then slowly turn. Sparks arced from the ancient bearing, the embers burning me where they landed on exposed skin.

"No!" Brent shouted.

I could hear him scrambling upward. He began crying, panic lacing his voice. His feet pounded against the thin metal of the fan housing as he tried to climb.

Then the fan quickly spun, metal grinding against metal. The light in the crawlspace dimmed. I looked back to see the crack close itself as the airflow increased. I could feel the breath being drawn out of my lungs. The force of the suction generated by the fan tugged at me. I dug my fingers into the cracks between the stones and held on for dear life.

The fan shook and rumbled. Bucking, several mounts broke free from the floor, and a raging cacophony suddenly replaced the roar of the fan before the blades came to an abrupt stop.

The drip drop of something wet trickling to the bottom of the fan told me everything I didn't want to know.

"Dig…" the voice said again, but it was farther away this time. I turned back to find the sliver of light had returned. Peeking out, I watched Bad Arnold meander into the mine opening and disappear inside. Slowly, the smoke receded from the holler, following the thing called Bad Arnold deep into the mine.

I hid there for days, staring through the small crack and expecting Bad Arnold to return at any moment. I don't know what ever happened to Danny. But Darlene… I was pretty sure what Bad Arnold had done to Darlene. Probably the same thing he'd done to Sadie. Her sobbing cries and screams echoed from the mouth of that fucking labyrinth for days, but there wasn't anything I could do.

I sat there, frozen for so long. I stared at this opening, praying that I'd wake up. *It had to be a dream*, I told myself. *It can't be real.*

But that was then.

The opening didn't look any different now. The chilly fall day even looked the same as it had all those years ago.

"Dig…" echoed from the maw of the mine.

I searched the ground for something, anything to use. Buried in the mud, I found a large piece of metal, a rock bar, that I wrenched free and wiped as clean as I could on the leaves.

"I'm not here to stare back at this damned abyss. I'm here to end this nightmare…"

I trekked into the cold, damp darkness for whatever awaited me.

"Dig…"

Dedication:

To missing and forgotten friends from the past. Life and time may have divided us, but the memories have never faded.

To that big-eared goofy kid who happily shared his *Dukes of Hazard* Hot Wheels with me on our first day of kindergarten all those years ago. Even after I left the hills and got busy with life, I never forgot ya or all the crazy things we did, buddy.

Dedicated to:

Brent A. Thompson
September 24, 1976 ~ February 27, 2021

Roc-ed

"You two better run! I'm going to get you! Rarr!" Both babies laughed and giggled as I chased them through the tall, uncut front lawn. For a change, I had the weekend off from work. No emails, no computer-glare, no pounding stress headache. For the first time in months, I could relax and enjoy my little family.

"You can't catch me, you can't catch me," Ilene's tiny voice sang. She laughed and teased and let out an ear-piercing little girl squeal.

"Now I've got you. You can't escape the claw! Rarr!"

"Ha ha, Dada! Hehehe," Dillon chuckled. "Stop Dada, stop it!" I tickled his belly and he thrashed about. "Stop it Dada," he laughed, then fell to the ground as a ball of giggly two-year-old.

"I'll save you Bubby," Ilene shouted and laughed. She jumped onto my back and clamped her arms around my neck. Almost at once, I began to choke.

"Lunch will be ready in a few minutes," my wife announced from the front door.

"Okay, Mommy," the children chimed.

"We'll be right in honey." I coughed, then peeled Ilene off of my back and sat her on the ground next to her brother.

"For a scrawny little princess you sure have a grip. Do you two want to play dinosaurs next? Roar, Roar, Roar!"

"No," Ilene replied with a wave of her hand. "Let's have a tea party."

"A tea Party? Bubby, do you want to have a tea party with Sissy," I asked.

"No," he said with a nod of his head.

"Oh Daddy, look, look, look! Daddy, look at that big bird in the sky," Ilene squealed.

"Yup, I see it honey," I replied without a glance. I gave Dillon a raspberry on his belly and tickled him again.

"Daddy," Ilene questioned. The tone of her voice had changed to something that sounded like uncertain fear. Both babies began to cry. Their faces contorted with the look of horrific, instinctual fear.

I was shoved toward the ground by something. I felt a sudden warm crunch, then nearly nothing.

With the same abruptness, the something jerked me away in the opposite direction.

I watched my beautiful children and the ground race away from me at rapid speed.

Something had me, but I couldn't move.

Only my eyes would obey. I felt a vise-like grip around my neck, but nothing below. I could not see what had snatched me, what had ripped me away from my babies. I could not see that thing that left them alone. That thing, that left them scared and unprotected. I could see nothing but my limp body as it dangled in the wind below.

Trees, houses, streets, and cars shrank away. The edges of my vision began to blur. I blinked to clear my vision, but darkness encroached.

I blinked again, the darkness grew. I blinked and felt a trickle of tears across my face.

I blinked…the wind buffeted my ears. I blinked…I felt nothing but cold tears. I blinked…but only the darkness remained.

We hope that you enjoyed this title and look forward to many more to come. Please, leave us a review! Reviews matter to all of our authors.

Take a look at some of our other award-winning series at https://threeravenspublishing.com/series-universes/

Visit us at https://www.threeravenspublishing.com and sign up for our newsletter for the latest and greatest news on upcoming titles and events.

Other series and titles you might enjoy.

JONATHAN MABERRY
EDITED BY: WILLIAM JOSEPH ROBERTS
& TIM "CAJUN" BISCHOFF
IT CAME FROM THE
TRAILER PARK
OPENING BY: MATT DINNIMAN
ELVIS
CONTEST
TONIGHT
TIKI BAR
STORIES BY:
CASEY MOORES - FRED PHILLIPS - G. SCOTT HUGGINS
JERRY HARWOOD - MEGAN MACKIE - MISHA BURNETT
ROBERT S. EVANS - SARAH ARNETTE
CHARLI COX - TIMOTHY HARDY
WILLIAM JOSEPH ROBERTS

DARIN KENNEDY
EDITED BY: WILLIAM JOSEPH ROBERTS & D. RHYEUS
IT CAME FROM THE
TRAILER PARK
STORIES BY:
CLARA MACGAUFFIN - RODNEY HATFIELD JR. - PHILIP K. BOOKER
DEWEY L. YEATTS - D.S. WATSON - ERICA BARNES - FRED PHILLIPS
JOE PALUMBO - MICHAEL CRAIG - TIMOTHY FRIEND

JOINT TASK FORCE
13
AMAZON
HOLDING THE LINE
BETWEEN HEAVEN AND HELL
13

B.E.N.T.
BIOLOGIC   ENHANCED   NASCENT   TALENT

THE RAVEN
AND
THE CROW
MICHAEL K. FALCIANI
FIND ME
ON AMAZON

STARFLIGHT

You can also keep up to date with our latest release announcements on <u>Scifi.radio</u> and get some of the best fandom programing on the planet.

Scifi for your Wifi

And don't forget to check out the latest edition of *Car Wars*

<u>http://www.sjgames.com/car-wars/</u>

Or the other amazing titles from
<u>Steve Jackson Games</u>

http://www.sjgames.com

…or the latest in the Car Warriors: Autoduel Chronicle fiction series.
https://threeravenspublishing.com/car-warriors-autoduel-chronicles/

www.ingramcontent.com/pod-product-compliance
Lightning Source LLC
Chambersburg PA
CBHW020048310726
48970CB00007B/2457